max from the planet of cool

written and illustrated by:

mcnall mason
and
max suarez

www.maxnmestudio.com

ISBN 978-0-9887499-0-0
published by MaxNmeStudio.com
Tacoma, WA

I have long wanted to write a children's book based on Max and the funny things he thinks and says but it wasn't until 2012 when, out of desperation to help Max adjust to a new school, I decided I was talented enough to do it.

In 2006, at the age of 4, Max did not have the verbal skills to participate in a conversation. He screamed if he was touched, showed zero affection towards anyone, joyously broke all his toys and had raging temper tantrums for unknown reasons. He also was not potty trained, still drank from a bottle and didn't sleep through the night.

That same year, Max's day care teacher clued me into Asperger's and a light bulb went off and I immediately took him to a specialist and removed gluten and dairy from his diet (both of which cost a lot of money and didn't help). SO - I bought all the books I could find written by people on the autism spectrum. I didn't care what the neural typical "experts" had to say, I wanted to know what grown-ups like Max had to say because it was the only way I could figure out how to learn to think like Max.

Little by little, as I dedicated the next 2 years of my life to working 1:1 with him, I learned how to communicate with him in ways he could understand and I slowly coaxed him far enough out of the fog of autism that he was able to function and learn.

In 2010, I started making art with Max as a project to raise money and awareness about autism as well as teaching him social skills. We made art wall hangings and hung them in galleries, at the Children's Museum in Olympia, at cafes and coffee shops in the Puget Sound area and won an honorable mention award at Seattle's Queen Anne Arts Walk in 2010.

By 2012, age 9, Max is main streamed in a classroom, does chores around the house, earns an allowance, watches YouTube videos about the interior design of airplanes (especially the 747's), walks the dogs, participates in everyday conversations, and tells me he loves me. I've been told, by parents of kids on the spectrum, that Max "passes" meaning it's not obvious he's autistic.

My goal in life is not to train the autism out of Max. I don't believe that's possible. My goal in life is to teach Max how to think and act like a neural typical person in the same way I would teach him another language if English wasn't spoken in our home. Autistic people are amazing and bring amazing skill sets to their life and can drill down on topics and achieve a level of competency that I can only dream of. I believe they can learn the social part once they understand why it matters.

We moved this year and it's been a torturous transition at school and especially with making new friends. In the midst of that chaos, I watched Max begin to retreat, not into the fog of his toddler years, but to a place of anger and acting out.

Not knowing what else to do, I turned to art and used it to turn his life into a book. Max really does think he comes from another planet where everything is made out of concrete and glass. It's a planet full of skyscrapers and moving sidewalks and force fields and seas full of Hansen's brand Mandarin Lime soda and girls are not allowed.

Max helped write this story, he helped design the elements, choose the characters, colors, and he specifically designed the teapot house which is our rendition of Bob's Java Jive, a building not too far from our new home. Every morning as he was eating breakfast we'd go over the pages and talk about the next ones and it made it a little easier for him to go off to a new school.

Through the process of writing this book and the two others we've now written, and working diligently with the school for 3 months, Max has finally adjusted to his new school and is no longer a behavior problem. (whoo-hoo!)

This book is the first in a series of seven books called: Magic Friendships and how they start. Each book raises money for charity. Thank you so much for supporting us!

Dedicated To:

UNCONDITIONAL LOVE

Max, Max
the new kid at school
told us he came from
the planet of cool

we all gathered round
on a big patch of grass

what i heard as he told us
his mixed up wild tale

made me think
he was crazy
like a blue
tailed big
snail

and that's pretty crazy

They were with Max
and wanted to stay
so I finally decided
to join them today

and oceans all filled
with orange soda pop

plus force fields all 'round
making outsiders stop

STAY OUT!

and then he told us
more and more

about this place
he's homesick for

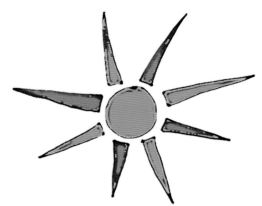

but i couldn't help it
i actually did

but please don't tell anyone

but i could not stop thinking this thought...

is max an alien astronaut

maybe he isn't
so weird after all

maybe he's normal and
likes to play ball

and later that night
when my room was
all calm

and i could quietly
hear the distant
voice of my mom

i lay in my bed and thought how it'd be to travel and see what max likes to see

i wondered what
i'd be able to see
in a land with no plants
not even a tree

Can you imagine what
they would eat for a meal
on a planet without girls
WHERE everything's real

or maybe they drink
their orange soda pop sea
all the soda you want
and all of it free

FREE SODA

SEA

We flew so far and
traveled fast
stars and galaxies
rushing past

so many magical
things to do
like flying over
mountains made
of blue goo

and listening to star songs
we clearly heard
while quietly flying
with never a word

i woke up up coZy in my bED
thinking 'bout things
max had said

and on my way
to class today
max was dressed
in astronaut grey

he smiled as we
walked to school
and talked about
his planet cool

and **that's how**

magic friendships start

As of December 2012, Max 'n Me have written and illustrated 3 books! Here are some of the characters we've come up with and places they go in our little corner of the world... which we affectionaltely call "Big D". The "D" stands for difference because this project is making a difference in our lives and our relationship to autism AND the proceeds are making a Big D for charities! It's all good!

visit us at www.maxnmestudio.com

SCHOOL   SHIP   PLANET OF COOL   LUCY'S HOUSE   ART STUDIO   PLAY HOUSE

BLUE TAILED SNAIL   LUCY   MAX   TIMMY   JIMMY   BIM   SUE

BIG BLUE   BILLY JUNE   MOON   MORGAN   GRAM BOL